Beauty and the Beastly Children

by Michael O. Tunnell ◆◆ pictures by John Emil Cymerman

Tambourine Books  New York

To Heather, Holly, Nikki, and Quincy—
the not-so-beastly children
M.O.T.

To the little beasties,
Jonathan and Laura
J.E.C.

Text copyright © 1993 by Michael O. Tunnell
Illustrations copyright © 1993 by John Emil Cymerman

Library of Congress Cataloging in Publication Data

Tunnell, Michael O. Beauty and the beastly children/by Michael O. Tunnell;
illustrated by John Emil Cymerman.—1st ed. p. cm.
Summary: After the love of Beauty turns him from a Beast into a
handsome prince, Auguste fails to reform the bad habits of his past
and sees the spell passed on to his three sons.
[1. Fairy tales.]   I. Cymerman, John Emil, ill.   II. Title.
PZ8.T87Be 1993 [E]—dc20 92-36757 CIP AC
ISBN 0-688-12181-0 (trade).—ISBN 0-688-12182-9 (lib. bdg.)
10 9 8 7 6 5 4 3 2 1
First edition

ost folks know the story of Beauty and the Beast—or at least they think they
do. Oh, they know about Beauty taking old bristle-face into her arms and promising
to marry him, just in time to keep Mr. Beast from croaking. And most people know
that the Beast was transformed into a rather nice-looking prince. And that the castle
suddenly changed from a dank and gloomy fortress into a place worth coming home
to. And finally, that Beauty and her new love (his real name was Auguste) were
married and began to live happily ever after. Yes, most folks think that's the end of
the story—but it's not!

It didn't take Beauty long to figure out that calling her Beast by the name Auguste hadn't changed anything. He was still pretty beastly. Oh, he didn't eat like a dog anymore or howl at the moon. Yet Auguste soon showed that he was still vain, proud, and just a little bit unkind—the very reasons the fairy had cursed him in the first place. Maybe his behavior had something to do with being crowned king (which must have gone to his head), for suddenly Auguste didn't seem to have time for anyone but himself.

"Beauty, old girl," he said, a smirk on his lips, "I can't go with you to visit your father tonight, though I hope his fever breaks. I'm guest of honor at the Enchanted Forest Archers' Club banquet. Last minute invitation, you know. Besides, a king cannot risk his health by visiting sick people."

Auguste stayed away from the castle more and more often to hang around with the neighborhood princes and dukes. He'd be gone for days on wild hunting parties that never resulted in any meat for the larder, only red eyes and sagging faces from too little sleep and too much ale. "A king must mingle with his subjects," he'd call to Beauty on his way out the door to play darts and other games of chance with the royal gang. Then he began to ignore his kingly duties. He stopped taking time to listen to the poor farmers and townspeople who came to the court with their problems.

He ignored the beggars who haunted the streets of nearby towns.

But finally Auguste went too far. The day Beauty gave birth to their first child, Auguste sent a message: "Hope it goes well. I must preside over the Interkingdom Jousting Tournament. A king's duty, you understand."

Beauty was furious. "The cad!" she cried. "Tricked me into marrying him with a fake dying act, no doubt," she gasped through clenched teeth.

At that moment the day grew as dark as a moonless night. Suddenly lightning ripped the blackness, thunder rattled the castle, and then not one but three babies entered the world.

It was so dark that the Interkingdom Jousting Tournament was canceled and Auguste, who was always a bit frightened of lightning, decided to hurry home rather

than go to the tavern with the royal gang. All along the murky forest path, Auguste thought he heard voices. Suddenly, he saw the fleeting figure of an old woman peeking from behind this tree, then the next. Her face was somehow familiar. And then he remembered.

"Egad!" Auguste screamed, and he raced pell-mell for the castle, feeling his face and staring at his hands all the way. He stumbled up the great stone staircase, snatching a lighted candle from its sconce. Ignoring Beauty and his new triplets, Auguste rushed through his bedchamber and began examining himself closely in a huge mirror with a gilded frame.

"Is my hair thicker? Yes, I think I see more hair! And my nose! Oh, no! My nose is longer. It's stretching! I saw her again, Beauty. In the woods. The old woman who changed me into a beast."

"You're as handsome as ever, you twit," Beauty said. "It's your three children you should be worrying about."

"Three? Three!" Auguste crowed and puffed his chest like a rooster. "I say, only a king of my fame and mettle could have performed such a feat."

"Auguste," Beauty said sadly, "please stop being an oaf and come look at your children. We are not done with your curse."

Auguste crept closer and peered into the crib. "Egad!" he screamed.

One of the baby boys had paws for hands and feet. Another waved a long, bushy tail. And the third yawned, showing a ferocious set of fangs. All three seemed rather hairy for newborn babies.

"It's all your fault, you . . . you . . . BEAST!" wailed Beauty. "Didn't learn a thing

from the first curse, did you? Selfish! Thoughtless! And now the curse has been passed on to your children."

Even Auguste could see that all this was true, though his first thought was to blame someone else. But then he made the mistake of thinking twice. "It's not my fault! It's that fairy. I haven't done a thing to deserve this," he cried.

Over the next few weeks, the babies—since named Athos, Porthos, and Aramis—grew and changed more quickly than wolf cubs. They were soon covered with thick, coarse hair. They learned to walk, run, and climb months earlier than any normal human child. Yet, as beastly as they looked, only Athos loped on paws, only Porthos carried a tail, and only Aramis snapped with fangs. But all three acted equally beastly!

Nothing in the castle was safe. The three untamed princes raced and tumbled down every hallway and staircase. They nipped at the servants' heels and bit the palace guards.

The cooks ran screaming when their kitchens were attacked by the terrible triplets. No dog or cat could be found within miles of the castle grounds. Athos, Porthos, and Aramis had frightened them away. (Untrue as it was, the townspeople whispered that the beastly children had eaten them.)

Local farmers lived in fear that the three would stampede their cattle and sheep, which they did regularly. Beauty could not control the trio, and Auguste did not try. He hid out with the royal gang so much of the time that he had no firsthand knowledge about the way his beastly children behaved.

But one day Auguste wandered home early, before the beastly children were down for the night. "Egad!" Auguste screamed as he approached the castle gate. He had spotted Athos swinging from the weather vane atop the tallest castle turret and grabbing at the pigeons. Just below their brother, Porthos and Aramis were chasing the pigeons along narrow ledges. On a nearby rooftop, Beauty and the nursemaids were begging the children to come down. The captain of the palace guard tried ordering the little beasts to fall in and stand at attention—until he realized that *fall* was not the best word to be using. But none of the begging or yelling did any good, for the fairy's spell had forced the beastly children to heed no one other than their shiftless father.

Auguste rushed up the flights of winding stairs to the roof where Beauty stood looking up at her children.

"Athos," he called sternly. "Come to me this instant. Porthos, Aramis. Come here."

It was a miracle! Athos dropped from the weather vane and tumbled into Auguste's arms. Porthos and Aramis leaped from the ledge, and each clung to one of Auguste's legs. Even Beauty's mouth dropped open in surprise (though she quickly began to see the clever fairy's plan). But no one was more surprised than Auguste, for the wild boys hardly knew him and had seldom heard his voice.

Getting the beastly children settled in for the evening had never been so easy as it was under the hand of Auguste. He managed to keep them from eating their supper like wild dogs. He was able to bathe them without calling in most of the servants to stand guard at the doors or to help hold the little creatures in the tub. And he put them to sleep in record time by telling the story of a wonderful prince who had also looked like a beast.

"Can't make it tonight," Auguste announced to the royal gang the next day. "The boys need me," he said to Beauty, who wisely said nothing. "A king's duty is to raise princes who will make fine kings, you know."

Whenever Auguste left for more than an hour or two, Athos, Porthos, and Aramis would terrorize the castle. "They simply need the strong hand of a father and the wise instruction of a king," he said, proudly. And, of course, Beauty wisely agreed.

Soon, the royal gang stopped coming by for Auguste, because he seldom left the castle. Instead, he spent time listening to his subjects, who drifted back to the king's court with their problems. Stories spread throughout the land about how the beastly children played quietly at their father's feet while he held court. Beauty and Auguste became known as the kindly queen and king, for they ruled fairly, solved problems quickly, and worked diligently to keep anyone in the kingdom from suffering. In time, the streets hosted not a single beggar.

Auguste stopped looking in mirrors and hardly ever boasted. Beauty finally found the Beast she had learned to love within the man Auguste. And as the days passed, Athos, Porthos, and Aramis grew gentle and quite civilized under the care of their father and mother. With each day, the three seemed a bit less hairy. Athos's paws began to look like hands and feet. Porthos's tail grew smaller and smaller. Aramis's fangs became shorter and more rounded.

Then, exactly one year after Athos had been lured from the weather vane, Auguste and Beauty, along with the semibeastly children, were holding court. The bent form of a woman in a tattered black hooded cape came forward to speak with the king and queen.

"Yes, old mother?" asked Auguste, as the hood fell away from the woman's face.

"Egad!" he murmured. "It's you. Whatever have I done this time?" The old face cracked into a rather charming four-toothed smile.

Suddenly, the day grew as dark as a moonless night. Lightning ripped the
blackness, thunder rattled the castle, and an old voice screeched, "Time's up!"

The sun sprang to life. The old fairy was gone, but it was plain to see that Athos had real hands and feet, that Porthos was missing a tail, that Aramis smiled a regular smile, and that the only hair to speak of was on top of the boys' heads.

E
T

Tunnell, Michael O.

Beauty and the
   beastly children.

$14.93

DATE			
34			
OCT 18			

BAKER & TAYLOR BOOKS